FOXY TALES

Caryl Hart AND Alex T. Smith

ALF...

...XY

A DIV...

First published in Great Britain in 2014 by Hodder Children's Books

FIRST EDITION

10 9 8 7 6 5 4 3 2 1

Design by Alison Still

A catalogue record for this book is available from the British Library

978 1 444 90932 6

Printed and bound in Great Britain by CPI Group (UK) Ltd, Croydon, CR0 4YY

The paper and board used in this paperback by Hodder Children's Books are natural recyclable products made from wood grown in sustainable forests. The manufacturing processes conform to the environmental regulations of the country of origin.

Hodder Children's Books
a division of Hachette Children's Books
338 Euston Road, London NW1 3BH
www.hachette.co.uk

Foxy DuBois and Alphonso Alligator

in:

The Road to Fame and Fortune

Introducing Foxy DuBois

She's smart. She's cute.

And she'll do anything
to get rid of Alphonso.

and Alphonso the Alligator

He's mean.
He's hungry.
And if Foxy doesn't feed him he's going to eat HER!

and Tony Ravioli

He's...err... he's the barman.

and Enzo Ravioli

Caterer to the Stars.

Looks just like Tony – but isn't.

and Special Guest
Mr Billy Bongo
as Mimi

Yep, he's cute.

DISCLAIMER:

No animals were humiliated, teased or eaten in the production of this book.

WARNING:

Contains scenes of excessive bodily gas, a rubber corset and an extremely large, warty bottom which some readers may find distressing.

Foxy DuBois' parents were rather posh and she was brought up loving the finest things life could offer. Her real name is Foxissima Ferrari Precious Pumpkin O'Leary Bigtwistle Bushy-tail DuBois the Third, but in the shady underworld she now inhabits, she goes by the name of plain old Foxy. So what happened to turn Foxy's life of luxury into a life of hardship and toil? I'll tell you. Alphonso. That's what. That greedy alligator ate her out of house and home and if she isn't careful, one day he might eat HER!

Alphonso the alligator was born hungry.

Well, to be precise he hatched hungry. Of course, when Foxy first spotted a large, tasty looking egg on her doorstep, she was thinking of only one thing. Breakfast. Little did she know that inside that perfectly smooth shell was not a delicious yellow yolk good for dipping toast soldiers, but a despicable reptile. Alphonso may be a bit, well, intellectually challenged, but he knows better than to let Foxy out of his sight, because while Foxy is around, Alphonso gets FED.

Welcome to Vaudeville, a big town full of small, mostly insignificant people. And chickens. As you can see, it's starting to get dark, so it's high time you scurried home. You wouldn't want to be out on these streets at night. Oh no. You see, strange things happen around here. Take the Ritz Movie House over there. In a few seconds, two shadowy figures –

one large, one small – will burst through the back door and you absolutely do not want them to spot you, believe me. In fact, here they come now – and they're arguing. So run. Run away now, because that big one has some very, very sharp teeth and he's looking rather hungry...

Chapter 1

In which Foxy reaches for the stars and Alphonso reaches for his dinner

An enormous, ugly alligator burst through the door of the East Street Eazy Diner, sending the other customers scurrying for cover. He was arguing fiercely with a small fox, who would have

JUST LIKE MAMA USED TO MAKE!

been reasonably pretty had she not been scowling quite so hard.

'Why do you have to spoil EVERYTHING?!' moaned the fox. 'You made such a noise guzzling popcorn I could hardly hear the movie!'

'Me spoil everything? That's a laugh,' retorted the alligator. 'All your sniffing and snivelling – anyone would think it was a sad ending, not a happy one!'

'My whole life is a sad ending, thanks to you!' Foxy DuBois closed her eyes, and for a split second was back in the movie house.

'Oh, to be galloping across the desert with the dazzlingly dashing Ebenezer Jones by my side!' she dreamed. But Foxy DuBois was not living in a dream; her life was a living nightmare. The only person by her side was Alphonso, a stinking, rotten, greedy alligator whose demands for food had ruined the whole movie – just as he was ruining her life.

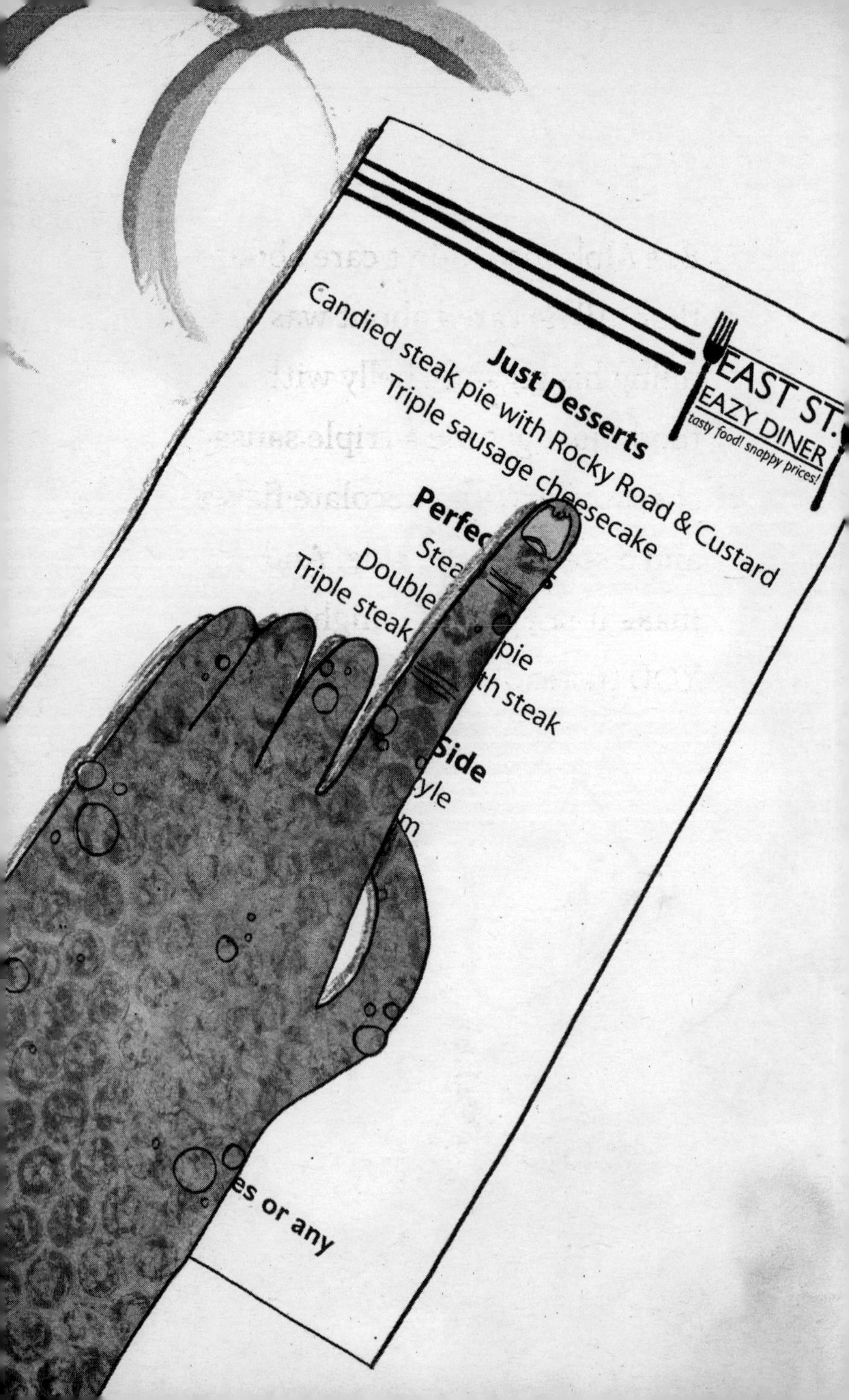

EAST ST.
EAZY DINER
tasty food! snappy prices!

Just Desserts

Candied steak pie with Rocky Road & Custard

Triple sausage cheesecake

Perfec

Stea s

Double

Triple steak pie

th steak

Side

yle

m

es or any

But Alphonso didn't care about that. All he cared about was filling his gigantic belly with food. 'Just get me a triple sausage cheesecake with chocolate flakes and a steak on the side. And make it snappy or I might eat YOU instead!' he sneered.

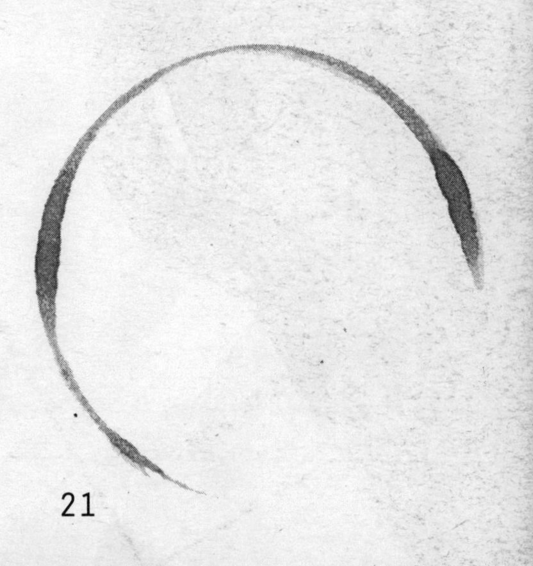

Tony Ravioli, owner of the East Street Eazy Diner, took the order and retreated to the kitchen. But when the food was ready, Foxy and Alphonso got the surprise of their lives. For there, loaded down with piles of overflowing plates, was not one but TWO Tony Raviolis!

'I'm so hungry,
I'm seeing double!'
gasped Alphonso.

The real Tony Ravioli plonked his plates on the table and put a proud arm round the other man's shoulders.

'Meet Enzo, my cousin,' he said. 'He's come all the way from Jollywood to see me.' The other Tony Ravioli took Foxy's paw, and kissed it gallantly. 'Enzo Ravioli, Caterer to the Stars, at your service,' he smooched. 'I hear you're a fan of my pal Ebenezer.'

'You know Ebenezer Jones?' gasped Foxy. 'That's incredible!'

FLAG
BUN
BACON
BURGER
RAW ONIONS

‘Sure I do,’ Enzo boasted. ‘Triple bacon burger with raw onions and a flag on top. I bet he’s first in the queue when I open up my burger van at the film studio tomorrow.’

‘Graah-snaawrr-crufumph!’ said Alphonso, which, roughly translated, means, ‘That’s amazing! I never met anyone who owned a real live burger van before!’

‘If you like,’ said Enzo smoothly, ‘I could get his autograph for you.’

Foxy's whiskers began to twitch. A sly smile spread across her foxy face. 'I'll get more than a measly autograph,' she thought. 'I'll persuade Enzo to take me with him to meet Ebenezer Jones in person! I'll sneak away in the dead of night, and by the time that infuriating alligator realises I've gone, I'll be far, far away on the road to fame and fortune! I'll meet all the stars! I'll go to parties and sip lemonade with Ebenezer Jones and I'll never ever be bothered by that hideous creature again.'

Foxy Du Bois

JOLLYWOOD

THE NEWS
FOXY HITS THE BIG TIME

JOLLYWOOD NEWS
EXCLUSIVE: FOXY GOSSIP!!!

AND THE Winner IS.
Foxy Du Bois!

Chapter 2

In which Foxy's dreams are rudely interrupted by a particularly nasty smell

'On the road at last.' Foxy DuBois sighed with contentment, as she and Enzo rumbled up the freeway. Early that morning, she had crept past the snoring Alphonso and snuck out of her shabby apartment block.

Then, keeping to the shadows like a criminal, she had scuttled over to the East Street Eazy Diner and begged Enzo to take her with him to Jollywood.

And now here she was, on the way to the land of her dreams – and not an alligator in sight. 'I've got away from that rancid reptile at last!' she chuckled. 'I'm free, FREE, FREE!'

Enzo smiled gallantly. 'I always fancied rescuing a beautiful damsel in distress.' he said. 'Maybe I could be your Prince Charming?'

'Oh, err, that would be lovely,' stuttered Foxy. But after a while, her nose began to itch. Her eyes began to water. 'What is that disgusting oniony-garlicky-baked-beany stench?' she gasped.

'Whoever smelt it, dealt it!'

Foxy jumped, making Enzo swerve the van dangerously. 'Alphonso!'

'What's he doing here?' snapped Enzo.

Mama Mia's
TOMATO
KETCHUP
FRAGILE!
THE
WOW!
THE HAPPY
HOT DOG
COMPANY

The alligator poked his warty snout through the window connecting the cabin to the rest of the van. He licked Foxy's ear lavishly with his long, green tongue, causing her to reel and gag at the putrid stench of his oniony breath. Then he took another lazy bite from the pile of frozen burgers he had found in Enzo's larder.

'Oh, you know me,' he grinned. 'I stick to Foxy like a piece of gum sticks to a shoe.'

Foxy turned back around in her seat and stared bleakly ahead.

This was not turning out like she'd planned.

Alphonso:
'Are we there yet?'
Foxy and Enzo:
'No!'
Alphonso:
'Can I drive?'

Enzo: 'Absolutely not.'
Alphonso: 'I need a wee.'
Country Music

Foxy: ‘You’ve only just been.’

Alphonso:
'I'm hungry! Feed me
or I'll eat you!'

Enzo: 'You can't be hungry. You've eaten three sacks of frozen chips, forty-five frozen burgers and a hundred and fifty frozen buns. I haven't got any food left!'
Alphonso: 'Are we there yet...?'
JOLLYWOOD

Chapter 3

In which Alphonso spies a tasty snack and Foxy dies tragically

After a very long, hot journey, the three weary travellers finally reached Jollywood. As they trundled past elegant pink buildings with turrets and palm trees, Alphonso yanked open the back door and dived out of the van.

‘Gimme that snack!’ he yelled.

He lumbered towards a group of chickens that were fussing around a smart, high-heeled woman as she lifted a tiny dog from her handbag.

Enzo slammed on the brakes, and before he could stop her, Foxy jumped out of the van and raced after Alphonso.

She rugby-tackled the ravenous alligator to the ground and sat on his head. 'That's not a snack!' she yelled. 'It's Mimi, the famous Jollywood Titchy Dog. He's doing a live movie shoot right now!'

'I don't care if it's King Kong,' snapped Alphonso. 'I want that snack and I want it NOW!'

'Listen, you dodo,' hissed Foxy, 'this could be my lucky break! I won't just mix with the stars, I'll become an actress! As soon as they notice my superior

performance skills, those people are bound to give me a *role*. Stay here and don't move.'

By now, a long queue of traffic had built up behind Enzo's van. He jumped out and tried frantically to wave them on, but was soon surrounded by revving engines and blaring horns.

Meanwhile, Alphonso paced impatiently back and forth, while Foxy:

flounced...

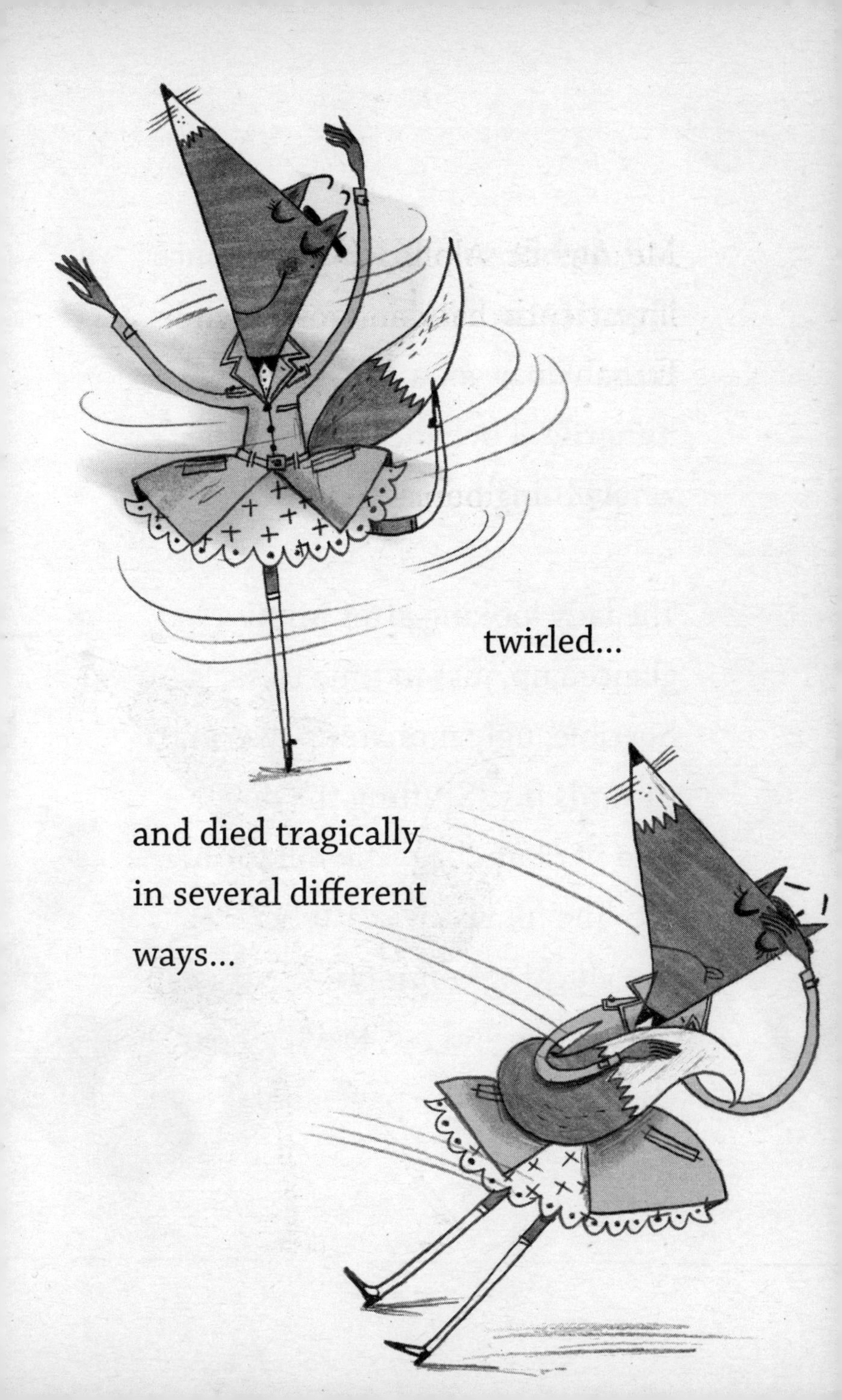

twirled...

and died tragically
in several different
ways...

But Alphonso was losing patience. 'Even if that double-crossing furball does get a *roll*,' he thought hungrily, 'I bet she just eats the whole thing herself.'

The lady looking after Mimi glanced up, just in time to see a horrible, ugly monster powering towards her. Stuffing the dog into her handbag, she ran for her life. The film crew scattered in a clucking commotion of feathers and fur, leaving Foxy, mid-pose, on the pavement.

'ALPHONSOOOO!'

She. Was. Furious!

'You bubble-brained banana!' she cried. 'You greedy gluttonous gremlin! You've frightened them all away!'

But Alphonso was mad too. 'You hogger of bread rolls!' he shouted. 'You tricky... err... fox!' They leapt at each other and tumbled down the street in a wild frenzy of kicking and punching – a dusty snowball of flailing arms and legs. They landed with a bump at the door of a huge grey building. The exhausted pair staggered to their feet.

POW!
OOF!
SLAP!

Right in front of them was
the infamous Studio One!

STUDIO
ONE

Chapter 4

In which Foxy hatches a plan to get rich quick and Alphonso falls for it. Again

Foxy's whiskers began to twitch and a sly smile spread across her foxy face. Studio One! 'This is it,' she thought. 'This is my chance to meet Ebenezer Jones. I'll go to parties. I'll sip lemonade. I'll live like a star!'

There was only one thing stopping her. Alphonso. That annoying animal could ruin everything with one flash of his teeth. She had to get rid of him. But how?

And then she saw it.

STUNT DOUBLE
REQUIRED TO TAKE
FALLS FOR FAMOUS
MOVIE STAR

Must be handsome, brave
and extremely gullible.
No qualifications needed.

ENQUIRE WITHIN

This company cannot be held responsible for any accident, injury or death occuring as a result of this employment opportunity.

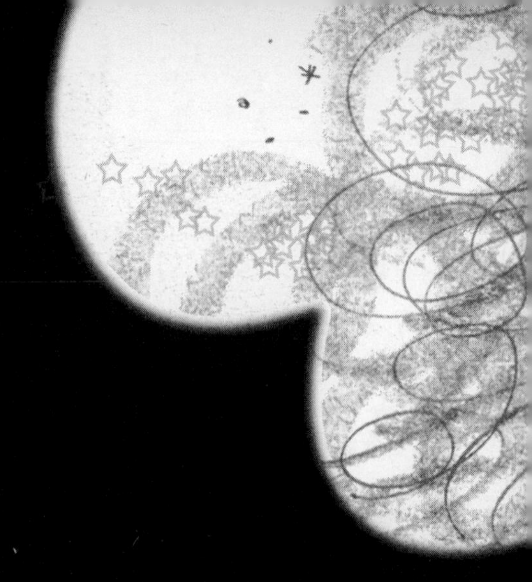

Foxy did a quick calculation in her head.

Gullible alligator + stuntman job = lots of money for Foxy to live like a star and impress Ebenezer Jones at showbiz parties.

Just then, Enzo screeched around the corner and jumped out of the van. 'Foxy, baby!' he fussed. 'Are you OK?'

'Enzo, darling,' she said smoothly. 'I've got some things to do, so shall we meet here later? If you feed Alphonso, maybe you and I could have a cosy cup of cocoa together?'

Enzo's eyes lit up. 'It's a date,' he said. 'I need to buy more burgers anyway. Your pet lizard has completely cleaned me out.'

With Enzo out of the way, Foxy got to work on Alphonso.

'Hey, buddy,' she said, 'you know how much you like eating? Well, Enzo would have to give you as much food as you wanted if you were a movie star.'

She pointed to the sign. 'If you sucked in your stomach and didn't actually talk, then you might just be in with a chance.'

'Is this another one of your tricks?' said Alphonso.

STUNT DOUBLE REQUIRED TO TAKE FALLS FOR FAMOUS MOVIE STAR

Must be handsome, brave and extremely gullible. No qualifications needed.

ENQUIRE WITHIN

This company cannot be held responsible for any accident, injury or death occuring as a result of this employment opportunity.

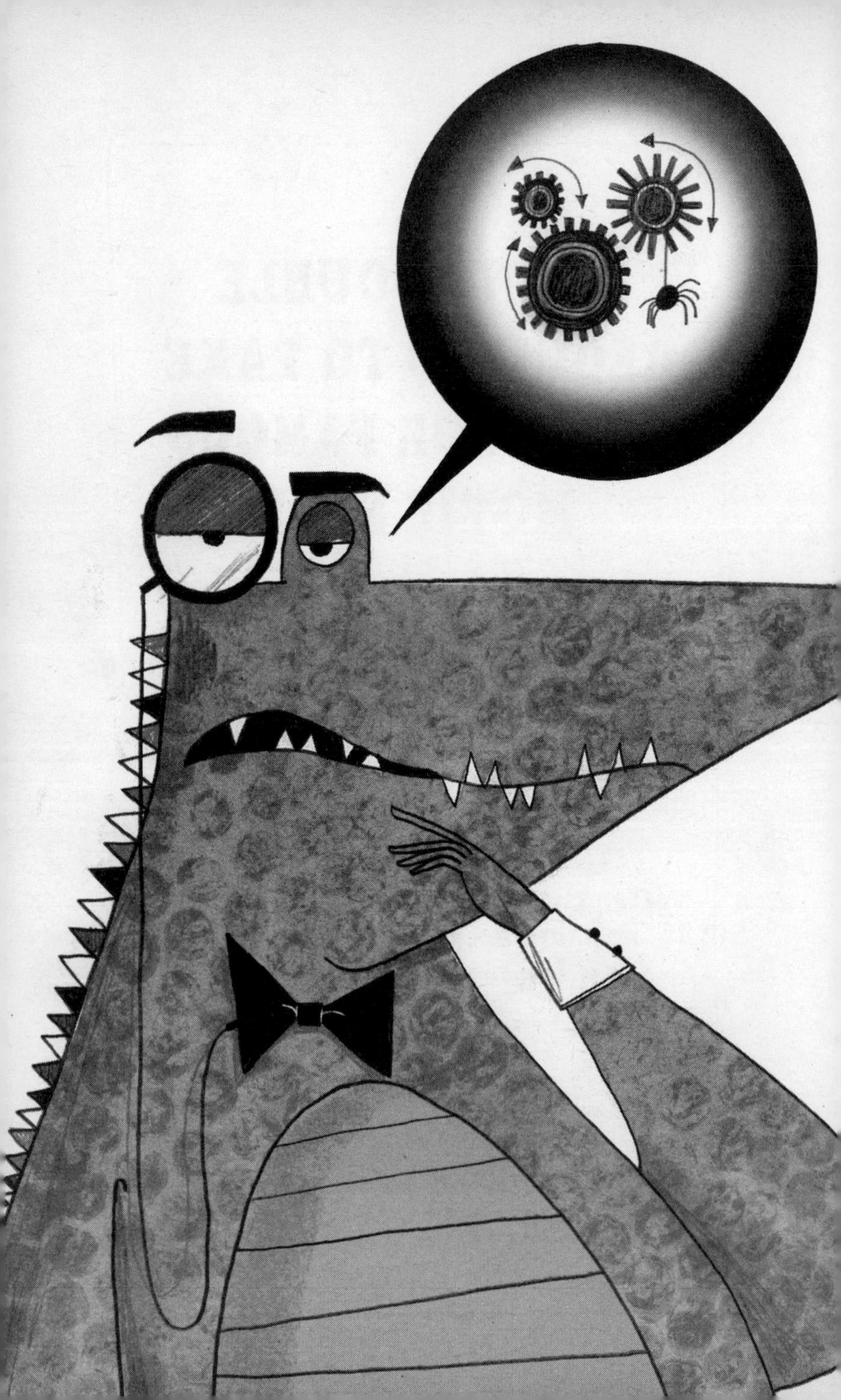

'Tricks? Me? Of course not!' gasped Foxy. 'But if you don't think you're good enough to be Ebenezer Jones's stunt double, and want to visit Enzo's burger van whenever you like, I suppose I could apply for the job myself…'

Foxy watched as the rusty cogs inside Alphonso's brain began to creak and groan. 'You mean, Ebenezer Jones doesn't jump off cliffs and crash cars and things himself?' he said.

'Of course he doesn't!' said Foxy. 'He gets someone to put on his clothes and do the dangerous stuff for him. Perhaps I will apply for the job...'

'Oh no you don't!' growled Alphonso. 'I'm going to be Ebenezer Jones's stunt double and YOU are not going to stop me!'

Foxy smiled a secret smile. This was going to be so much easier than she'd imagined.

Inside the studio, a group of people were sitting at the edge of a steep cliff made of wood, polystyrene and papier mâché. There were cameras and lights and microphones everywhere.

'G-good morning everyone,' said Foxy.

'We've c-come about the job. I'm Foxy DuBois from the DuBois Stunt Agency, and this is my client, Alphonso. He's not much to look at but he's very hard-wearing and extremely gullible.'

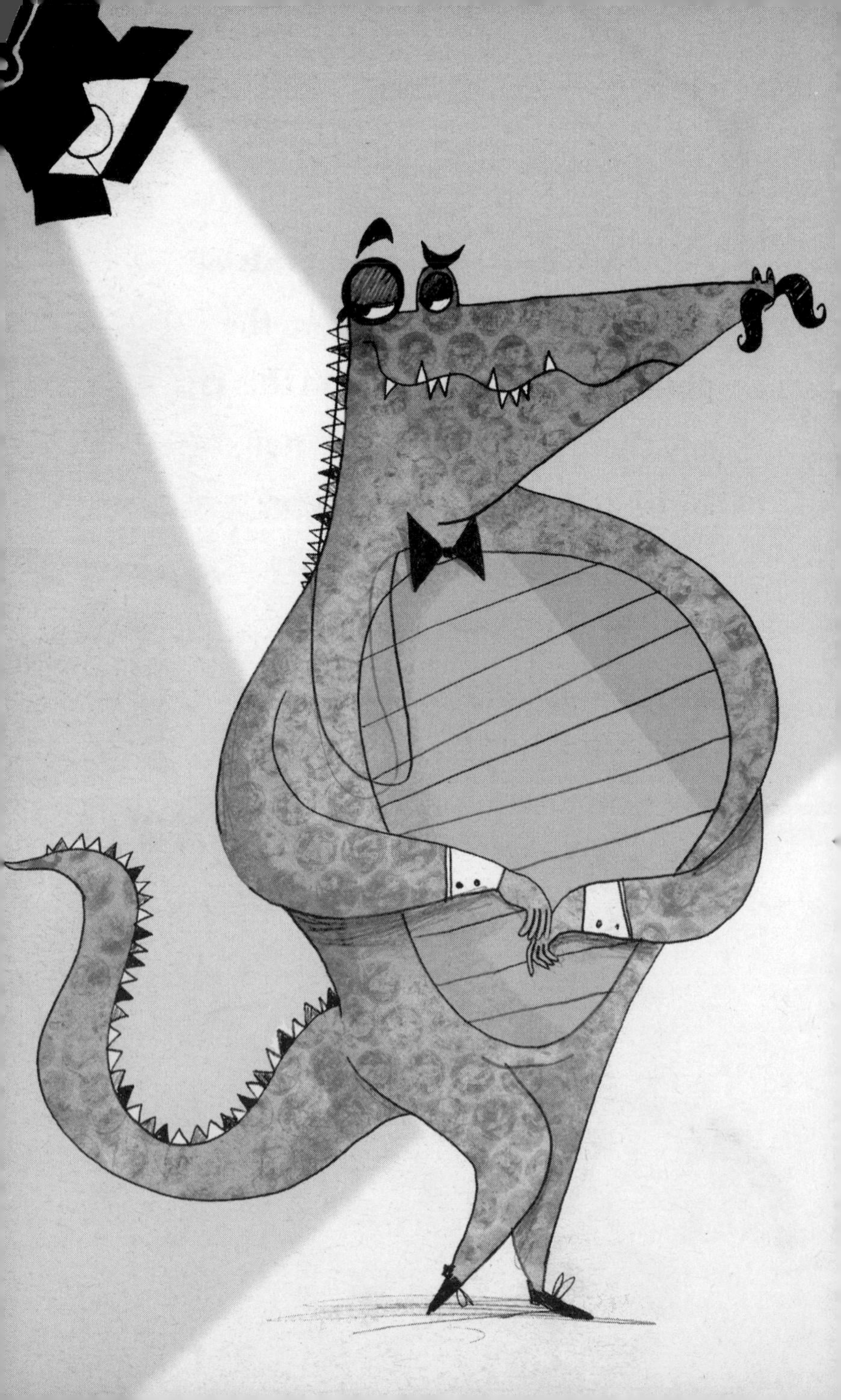

Alphonso sucked in his stomach and tried to look as gullible as possible, whatever that was.

A large, heavy-jowled bulldog looked critically at Alphonso. 'He's a bit on the large side,' he grumbled. 'And we'll have to airbrush out some of the uglier warts in post-production, but I suppose he'll do. Ebenezer, meet your new stunt double.'

Chapter 5

In which Alphonso goes for a dip and comes up trumps

'Oh, Mr Jones,' Foxy gushed as she pushed her way towards Ebenezer, 'how lovely to meet you. I'm such a big fan!'

Ebenezer Jones nodded briefly at Foxy before turning to the dog.

'But, Mr Bigshot, he don't look a bit like me!' he drawled.

'A bit of make-up here and there and you'll never know the difference,' said Mr Bigshot. He thrust a brown jacket, some trousers and a hat at Alphonso then pulled him towards the edge of the cliff. 'OK, Mr Alfuzz… Alfozz… err… whatever,' he barked. 'You're gonna put on those clothes, and when I tell you, you're gonna jump off the edge of this cliff and land in that river.

Then you flail around a bit, pretend to drown, till we come an' haul you out. Got it?'

Mr Bigshot walked away, leaving Foxy and Alphonso peering at the raging torrent below. 'What have you got me into?' gulped Alphonso. 'You know I can't swim.'

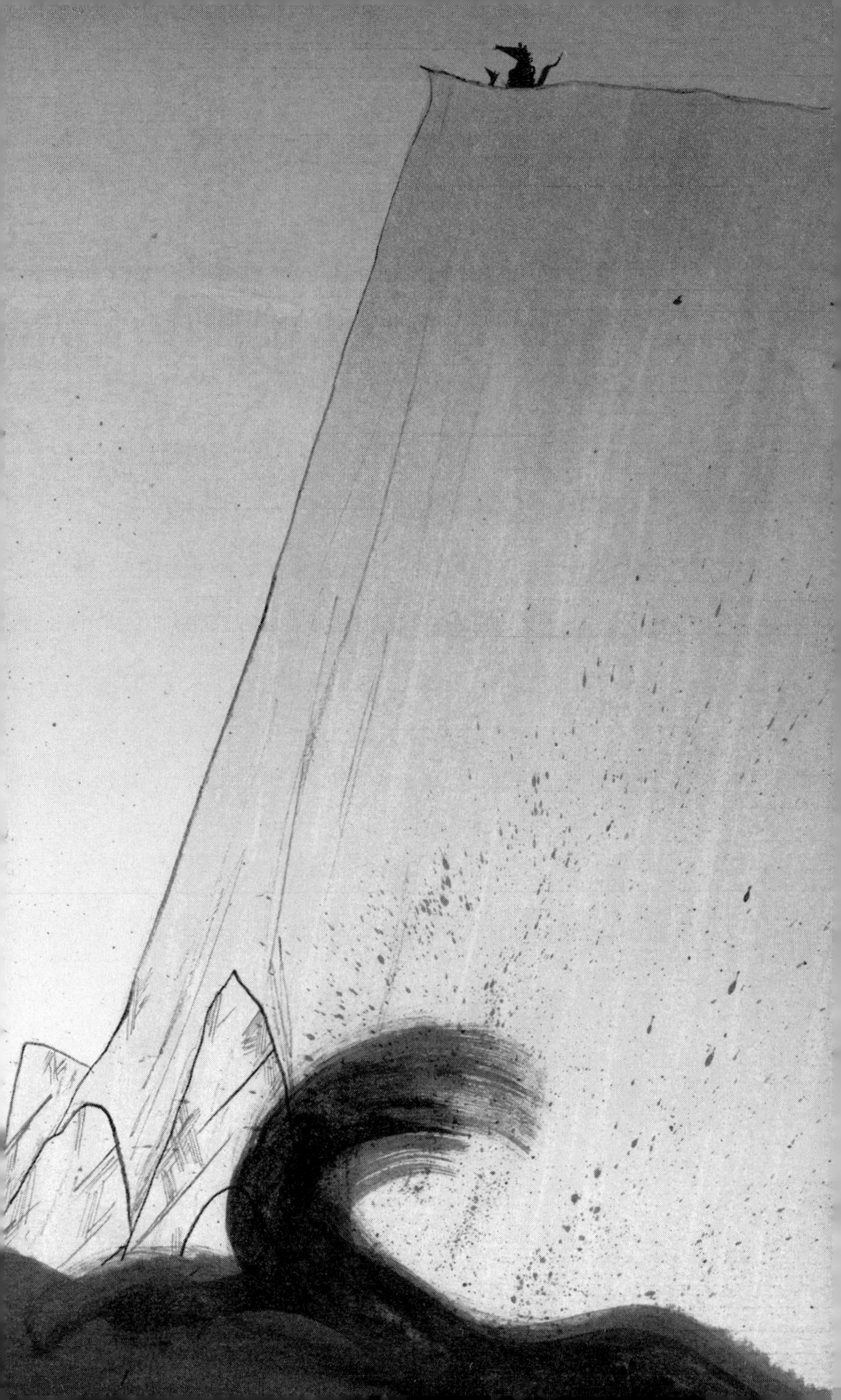

'Don't worry,' soothed Foxy. 'I'm sure it's perfectly safe. You'll probably have some waterwings hidden underneath your clothes. Just think of that super nosh-up waiting for you in Enzo's van when you've finished.'

A couple of hours later, with the cameras rolling and the film crew at the ready, Alphonso-dressed-as-Ebenezer-Jones threw himself off the fake cliff and plunged into the bubbling river far, far below. But instead of bobbing around safely, pretending to drown, Foxy watched in dismay as he simply sank beneath the waves, taking all her hopes and dreams with him.

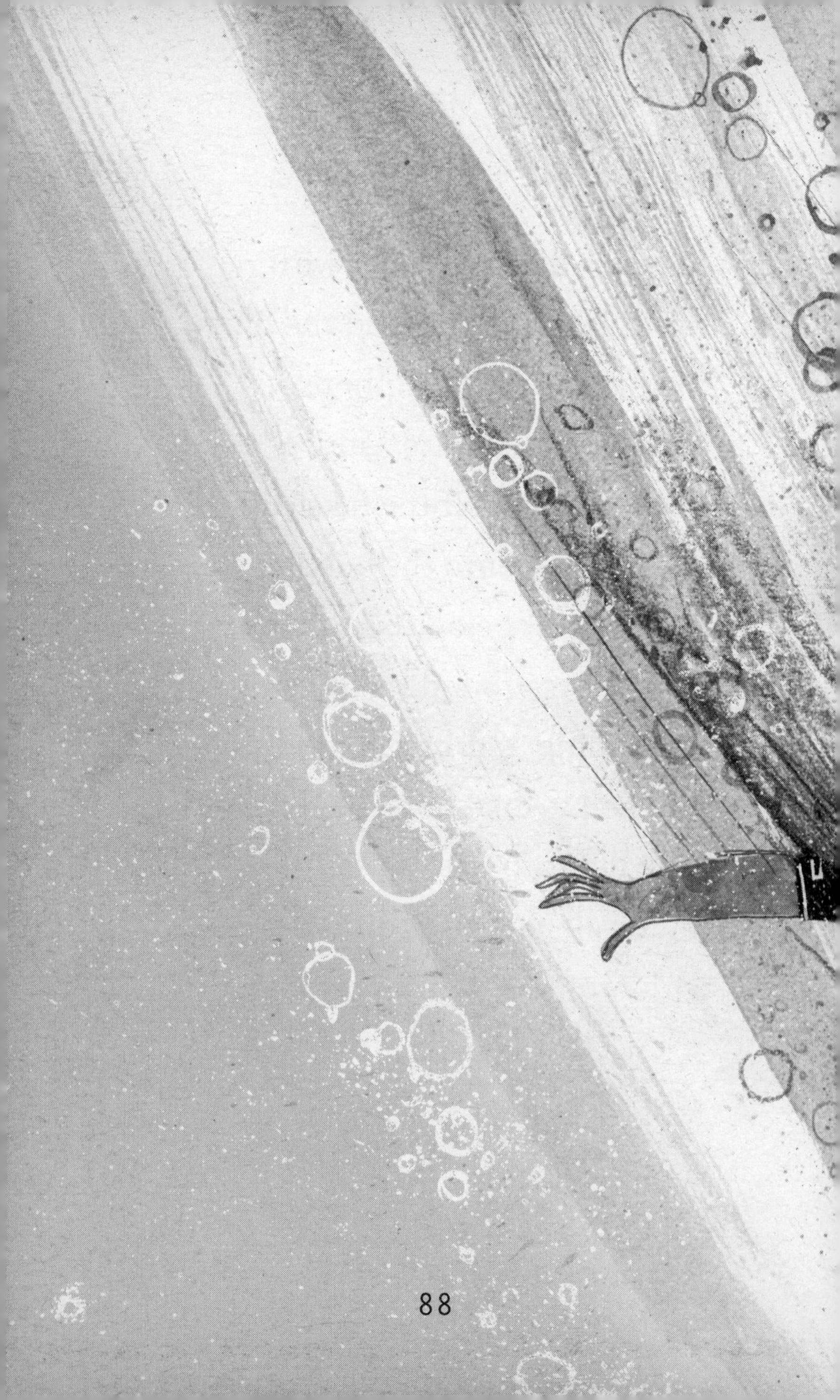

'Honestly,' she thought. 'I spend my whole life trying to get rid of that rancid reptile and the one time I actually want to keep him alive to make me some money, he goes and drowns on me. Typical.'

There was only one thing to do: use sympathy to get close to Ebenezer Jones. She squeezed out some fake tears and grabbed his hand. 'Oh, my precious Alphonso!' she cried.

Before Ebenezer could reply, an almighty rumble came from beneath the waves.

The huge build-up of burger-induced gas in Alphonso's stomach had suddenly let rip and he was propelled out of the river like a cork out of a bottle of very fizzy pop. He ploughed up the fake riverbank, skidded through a forest of potted cacti, and landed headfirst in a pile of film reels.

Mr Bigshot was delighted. 'That was fantastic, Alfuzz... Alfozz... err... whatever!'

He handed Foxy a bundle of bank notes and smiled broadly.

'Excellent job, Miss DuBois. I'll see you both tomorrow.'

Foxy beamed with
pleasure and relief
as she counted the
money and thought
of all the beautiful dresses
and ridiculous shoes she
would buy to impress Ebenezer
Jones. She turned to him for a
congratulatory hug...

...but the handsome actor had gone.

Chapter 6

In which Alphonso gets an invitation and Foxy, err... doesn't

That evening at the burger van, Enzo plonked a huge plate of pies on a table and called Alphonso over. The exhausted alligator collapsed in a plastic chair and started guzzling, pausing only to cough up waterweed or pick a cactus spine out of his nose.

Enzo kissed Foxy's paw lavishly, presented her with the promised cup of cocoa, and sat down next to her.

'That crocodile of yours is the talk of the town,' he said, gazing into Foxy's eyes. I heard Mr Jones is having a huge party in a couple of days to celebrate.'

He grabbed Foxy round the waist and pulled her close. 'We can go together,' he crooned.

Foxy coughed nervously and wriggled out of Enzo's arms.

'A party!' she gasped.
'How wonderful!'

'Oh yes,' said Alphonso. 'There was a notice in the dressing room. Everyone's invited.'

'Everyone?' murmured Foxy. Her mind raced. What should she wear? What if Ebenezer asked her to dance?

‘Well, everyone important,’ said Alphonso. ‘You know, actors, stunt-doubles, people like that.’ He paused to think. ‘’S funny though, I don’t remember seeing your name on the guest list.’

‘What!’ thought Foxy. This was not good. Not good at all. ‘I’m the one who should be dancing the night away in style, not that no-brained numbskull!’ she muttered. She pulled an eyebrow pencil from her pocket, grabbed a serviette and scribbled out a plan.

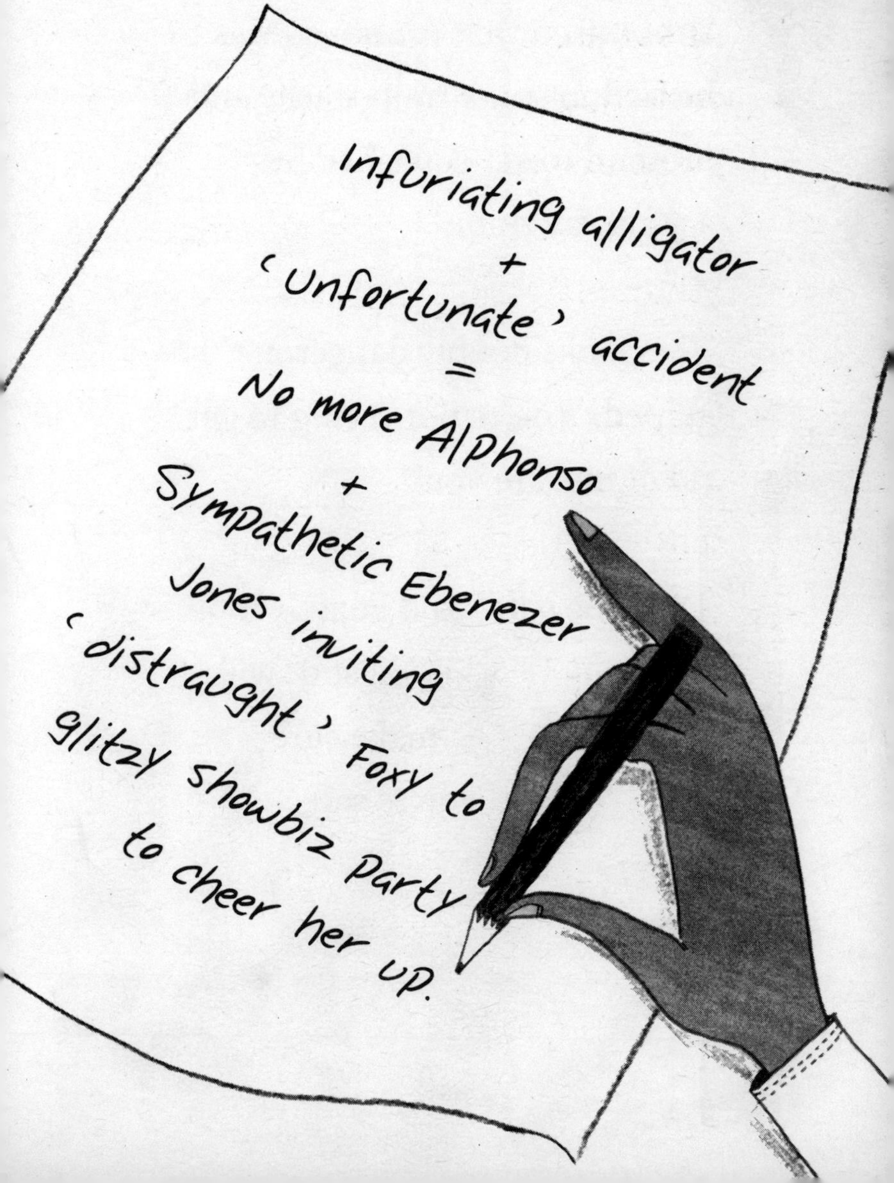

Infuriating alligator
+
'Unfortunate' accident
=
No more Alphonso
+
Sympathetic Ebenezer
Jones inviting
'distraught' Foxy to
glitzy showbiz party
to cheer her up.

The next day, Mr Bigshot announced that Alphonso was to be tied to some train tracks and pretend to get squashed by a runaway train.

'This looks doubly dangerous,' he gulped. 'You're not trying to get rid of me, are you?'

'Don't be silly,' said Foxy. 'Mr Bigshot will make sure you're safe.

And you can't let Mr Jones down when he's planning a party in your honour.'

'Enzo's cooking your favourite tonight – rotten fish sundae with green custard.'

At the mention of food, Alphonso's eyes lit up. He headed for the dressing room for his pre-stunt massage and manicure. Meanwhile, Foxy quickly swapped his armour-plated corset for another she had found – one made of rubber.

Then she looked for a lever on the tracks that would change the direction of the train, sending it hurtling towards Alphonso.

If her plan worked, he would end up like a toad on the motorway and Foxy would be on her way to a star-studded wedding with the gorgeous Ebenezer Jones.

'After a short period of polite mourning, naturally,' she thought with a smile.

An hour later, Alphonso-dressed-as-Ebenezer-Jones lay down on the train tracks and allowed the stagehands to tie his arms and legs with string. Mr Bigshot, Ebenezer

Jones and Foxy DuBois sat down in folding chairs to watch the scene.

When everything was ready, Mr Bigshot raised his hand and barked, 'Lights. Cameras. ACTION!'

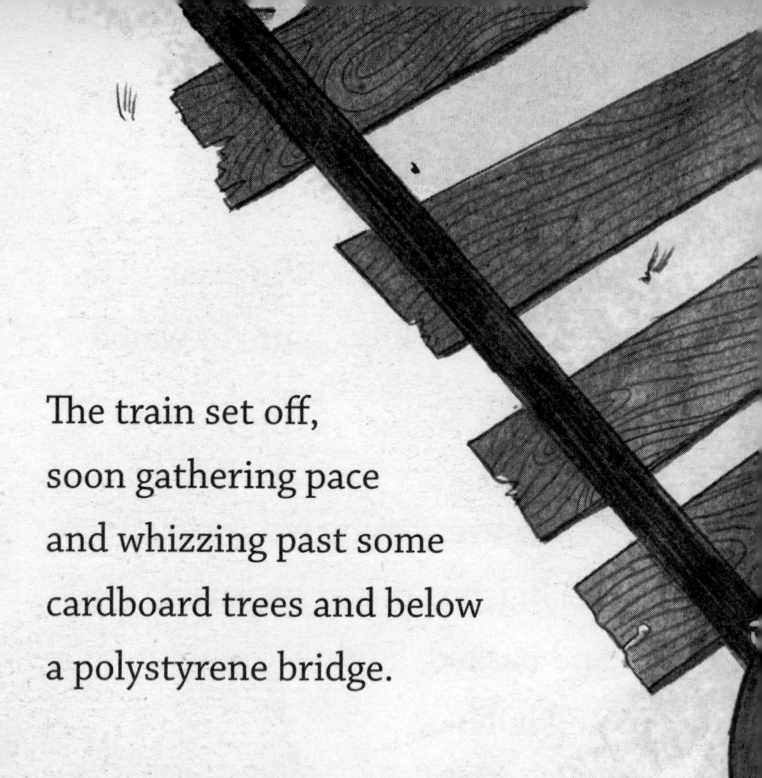

The train set off,
soon gathering pace
and whizzing past some
cardboard trees and below
a polystyrene bridge.

But instead of veering off away
from Alphonso, the engine
kept hurtling towards him. He
struggled to break free, but the
string around his wrists and
ankles was too tight.

Foxy DuBois, Mr Bigshot and Ebenezer Jones stared, mesmerised, as Alphonso-the stunt-double disappeared underneath the wheels of the roaring locomotive…

'This is it,' Foxy thought. 'I'll finally be rid of that useless alligator!'

Chapter 7

In which Alphonso is saved by his belly and shares a romantic dinner for two

The train was upon Alphonso. But the strangest thing happened. Instead of continuing along the line, squashing the alligator to smithereens, the train simply bounced off Alphonso's bulging rubber belly and shot back the way it had come!

'Dang, blast and bother it!' muttered Foxy. Her plan to get rid of Alphonso had failed!

But Mr Bigshot and Ebenezer Jones couldn't have been happier. They jumped to their feet, whooping in delight. 'BRAVO!' shouted Mr Bigshot. 'That was FANTASTIC!'

Seizing the moment, Foxy put on a coy smile and said, 'I'm glad you approve. I thought it would look SO much more realistic if the train was to actually hit him.'

'Miss DuBois,' said Mr Bigshot, thrusting more notes into Foxy's hands. 'Your idea to dress him in a rubber corset was GENIUS! I really can't thank you enough. Say you'll join me for a fancy dinner this evening?'

‘I’d be delighted,’ smiled Foxy. ‘Will Mr Jones be accompanying us?’

Ebenezer Jones shook his head. ‘No can do,’ he said. ‘Gotta pose for *Stars R Us* magazine tonight, but I guess you could come along to my party tomorrow, if you have nothing else planned.’

Inside, Foxy was bursting, but she kept her cool exterior. 'I'll check my diary,' she answered coyly.

Outside the studio, Enzo was waiting expectantly. His van was festooned with flowers and ribbons. 'Hey, beautiful,' he said as Foxy and Alphonso emerged. 'I've got a special treat lined up for you.'

'Oh, you shouldn't have,' said Alphonso, blushing.

Enzo gave him a puzzled look, then took Foxy by the arm and led her to a table made up with fancy crockery and candles. But Foxy was too flustered to sit down. 'Sorry, Enzo,' she said, waving the banknotes in his face, 'can't stop. Got to get to the boutique before it closes.

Need a new dress for the party tomorrow.' And off she rushed without a backwards glance.

As Enzo gazed longingly after her, Alphonso wedged his enormous bottom into Foxy's chair, tied a napkin around his neck and picked up his knife and fork. 'Never mind,' he said. 'You've still got me.'

Chapter 8

In which an unfortunate alligator plunges towards certain death while a scheming fox cries crocodile tears

The next day, Mr Bigshot announced that Alphonso would be jumping out of an aeroplane, which would be pretending to spiral out of control. 'This is the hardest stunt in the movie business,' he beamed. 'If anyone can do it, YOU can!' The entire crew set off in a convoy of buses for the airfield. Not one to miss a burger-selling opportunity, Enzo revved up his burger van and followed on behind.

The sky was criss-crossed with coloured smoke as stunt planes circled and dived and spiralled in the air. 'This is amazing,' said Foxy. She'd had a very posh dinner at the Terribly Grand

Hotel with Mr Bigshot the night before. Now she was smiling, dreaming of being swept across the dance floor by Ebenezer Jones.

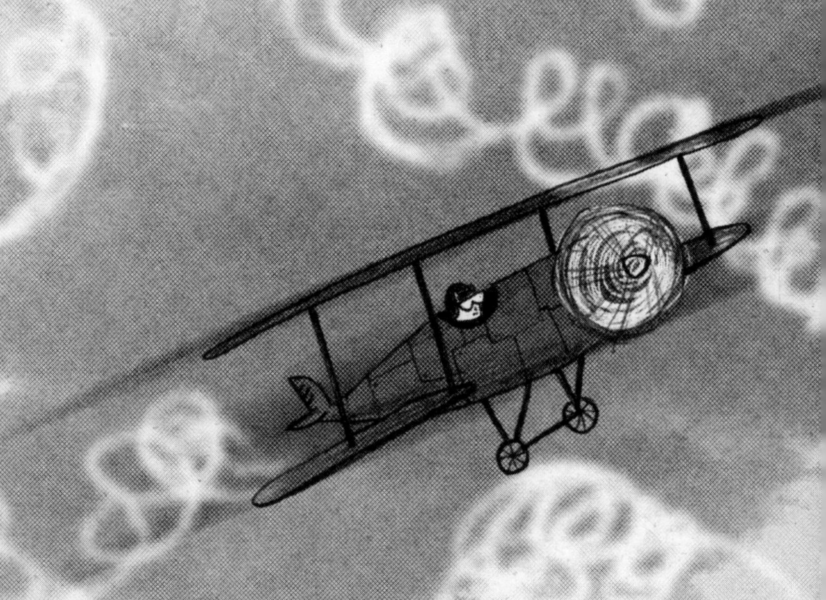

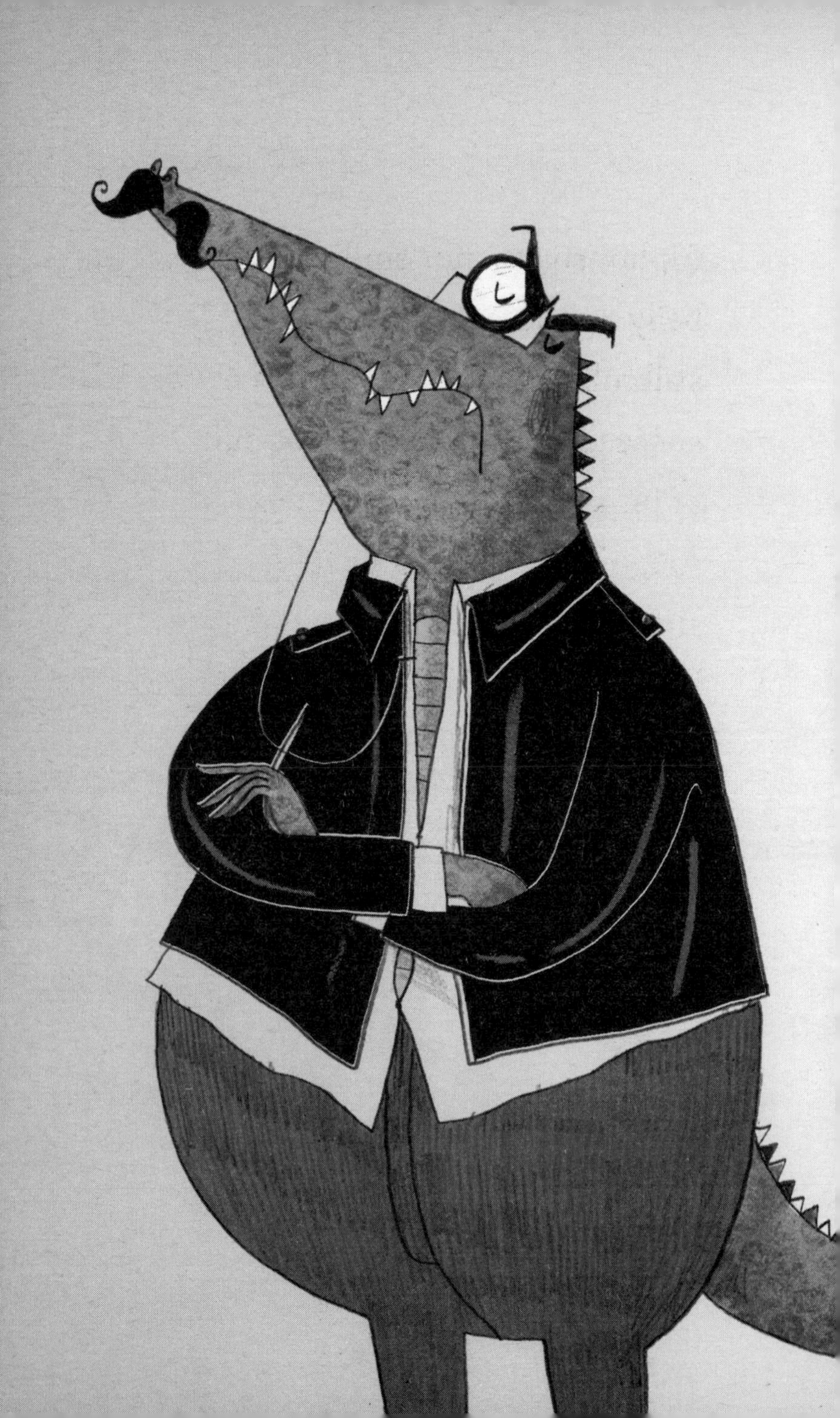

Alphonso was not smiling. His belly was sore, his ears were still full of water, and when he sneezed, cactus spines shot out of his snout. He grabbed Foxy roughly. 'I'm not doing it,' he snarled. 'You know I don't like heights.'

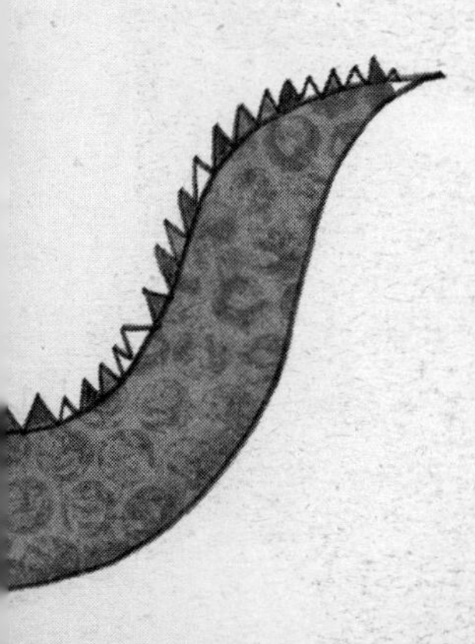

'Don't worry,' said Foxy. 'You'll be wearing a parachute so you'll be perfectly safe. Just think of all the lovely nosh at the party tonight. There'll be cheese and pineapple burgers on sticks, and prawn sausage cocktails and everything!'

'Hrmph,' grunted Alphonso, stalking off to the plane.

Foxy DuBois waved innocently as the stunt plane climbed into the blue Jollywood sky. 'Goodbye!' she called. Adding to herself, 'And good riddance!'

She could hardly contain her joy as Alphonso-dressed-as-Ebenezer-Jones jumped from the plane and plummeted towards the ground.

She held her breath when he pulled the rip cord, and grinned like a maniac as the parachute flopped sideways out of the bag and flapped uselessly around his ears.

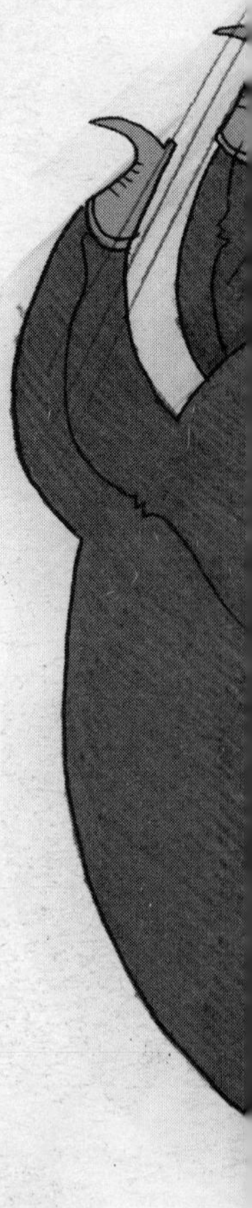

'Cutting those parachute strings had been so easy!' thought Foxy. 'Now for the cover-up.'

Foxy ran out into the field.
'Somebody do something!'
she screeched, dramatically.

'My
wonderful

Alphonso
is going to diiiiie!'

She threw herself at Ebenezer Jones and buried her face in his shirt, pretending to sob. 'Goodbye, Alphonso!' she wailed. 'Life will never be the same now you are gone.'

But when she peered out from underneath Ebenezer Jones's armpit, Foxy couldn't believe what she saw.

Just as Alphonso was about to spatter on the ground, a sudden gust of wind caught inside his parachute and pulled him back up into the air. Round and round he span, in a series of death-defying swoops and spectacular loop-the-loops.

‘Are we getting this, people?!’ barked Mr Bigshot. His cries of delight turned quickly to cries of horror. ‘He’s heading straight for us!’ he yelled. ‘Run for your lives!’

The last thing Foxy saw was Alphonso’s enormous warty bottom, hurtling straight towards her.

Then she was flung to the ground

and the whole world went black.

Chapter 9

In which Foxy's plan unravels, wraps itself around her ankles, and trips her up good and proper

As the dust cleared, Foxy sat up shakily, and took in the devastation around her. The air was filled with flashing lights and sirens as the emergency services attended the last, dazed members of the film crew. Alphonso sat on a rock, picking his toenails.

'Wh-what happened?' groaned Foxy.

'Well,' drawled Alphonso, 'it seems that somebody cut my parachute strings. I would have been dead if you hadn't arranged such a lovely soft landing. Mind you, Ebenezer Jones might regret using himself as a human shield to protect you from the impact. They say he might never recover.'

All the colour drained from Foxy's face, and her knees began to tremble. What had she done?

'By the way,' added Alphonso, 'Mr Bigshot knows it was you.' He looked up from his toenails, fixed his yellow eyes on Foxy and made a snipping motion with his claws.

'But – how did he find out?' Foxy gasped.

Alphonso raised his eyebrows meaningfully. 'So it was you then!' Alphonso tried to grab Foxy. 'I'll tear you limb from limb!' he snarled.

Foxy dodged sideways and crashed straight into Mr Bigshot, knocking him to the ground. 'Mr Bigshot!' she stammered. 'I'm so sorry.'

But the bulldog was not interested in Foxy's apologies. 'Why, you no-good, self-seeking, scheming FIEND!' he yelled. 'You have disabled my best actor, destroyed my film crew and ruined my movie! I'm going to shake you till your teeth rattle and then I'm going to feed you to a hungry hyena!'

He lunged at Foxy but was overtaken by an even angrier Enzo Ravioli. 'Foxy DuBois!' he cried. 'You are a double-crossing, two-timing, selfish temptress! How could you use me like that? Pretending to like me so I'd feed your disgusting pet when all the time you were sucking up to Mr Bigshot and canoodling with Ebenezer Jones.'

Foxy tried to protest but Enzo was not listening. 'Don't try to deny it, Foxy. I saw it with my own eyes – all that smooching and cuddling! It makes me sick!'

'I don't suppose there's any chance of a lift back to Vaudeville?' she asked.

‘Hey, Doll Face!’ beamed Tony Ravioli. ‘You’re back! How’d it go?’

Foxy and Alphonso collapsed into their seats, panting hard. ‘I bet you had a ball – all the lights and the stars and the costumes… and how’s my favourite cousin?’ He plonked an enormous pile of pancakes on the table which Alphonso guzzled greedily. Foxy said nothing.

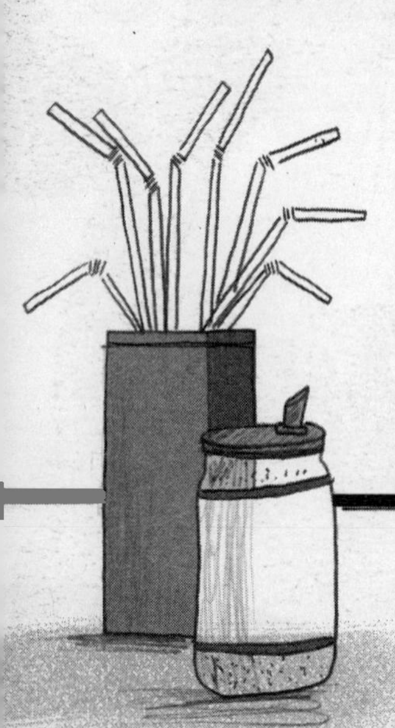

'Hey, cheer up, Blue-Eyes,' said Tony. 'How about you and me go to the Ritz Movie House to celebrate your homecoming?'

Foxy groaned and put her head in her paws. 'Thanks, Tony,' she muttered. 'But I've rather gone off movies. In fact,' she sighed, 'I never want to see another one ever again!'

The End

... Or is it?

Watch out for more Foxy Tales coming soon to a bookshop near you.

Foxy DuBois' Best Movie Guide

Stuck for something to watch? Don't worry, Foxy is here to tell you about her favourite films:

EBENEZER JONES AND THE THIMBLE OF DROOL

There's this handsome man who does lots of daring jumping around, beats up some baddies and rescues a beautiful, clever fox. The two fall in love and live happily ever after!

Rating: 10/10 for action, adventure, romance. There are no alligators in this movie.

KUNG-FU FOX

Action adventure movie about a beautiful, clever fox who becomes a Kung-Fu expert overnight and defeats all the baddies, including an alligator.

Rating: 9/10 Some good moves. Very educational.

FOXES IN THE CARIBBEAN

A wonderful, relaxing film about a beautiful, clever fox who lounges around by the pool in the sunshine all day and isn't bothered by any pirates. Or alligators.

Rating: 9/10 Ideally, this movie would be much, much longer. And in 3D.

UNTANGLED

A beautiful, clever fox is trapped in a tower by an evil alligator. Luckily, along comes the dashingly handsome Ebenezer Jones, who climbs up the fox's extra-long magic tail and whisks her away!

Rating: 10/10 Well, you've got to have a dream, right?

Essential Kit for Stunt Doubles

Would you like to be in the movies like Alphonso? You too could become a stunt double with this comprehensive stunt-double kit. Available from all good stores for not very much money.

1. Man-bag
2. Waterwings cushion to put in the seat of your pants
3. Snacks to eat between scenes (lots)
4. Sunglasses to shade sensitive eyes from bright studio lights
5. Plasters
6. Tweezers for picking out prickles, gravel and thorns in the sides
7. Self-adhesive scars (re-usable)
8. Super-strong make-up to hide those unwanted warts
9. Trowel for applying super-strong make-up

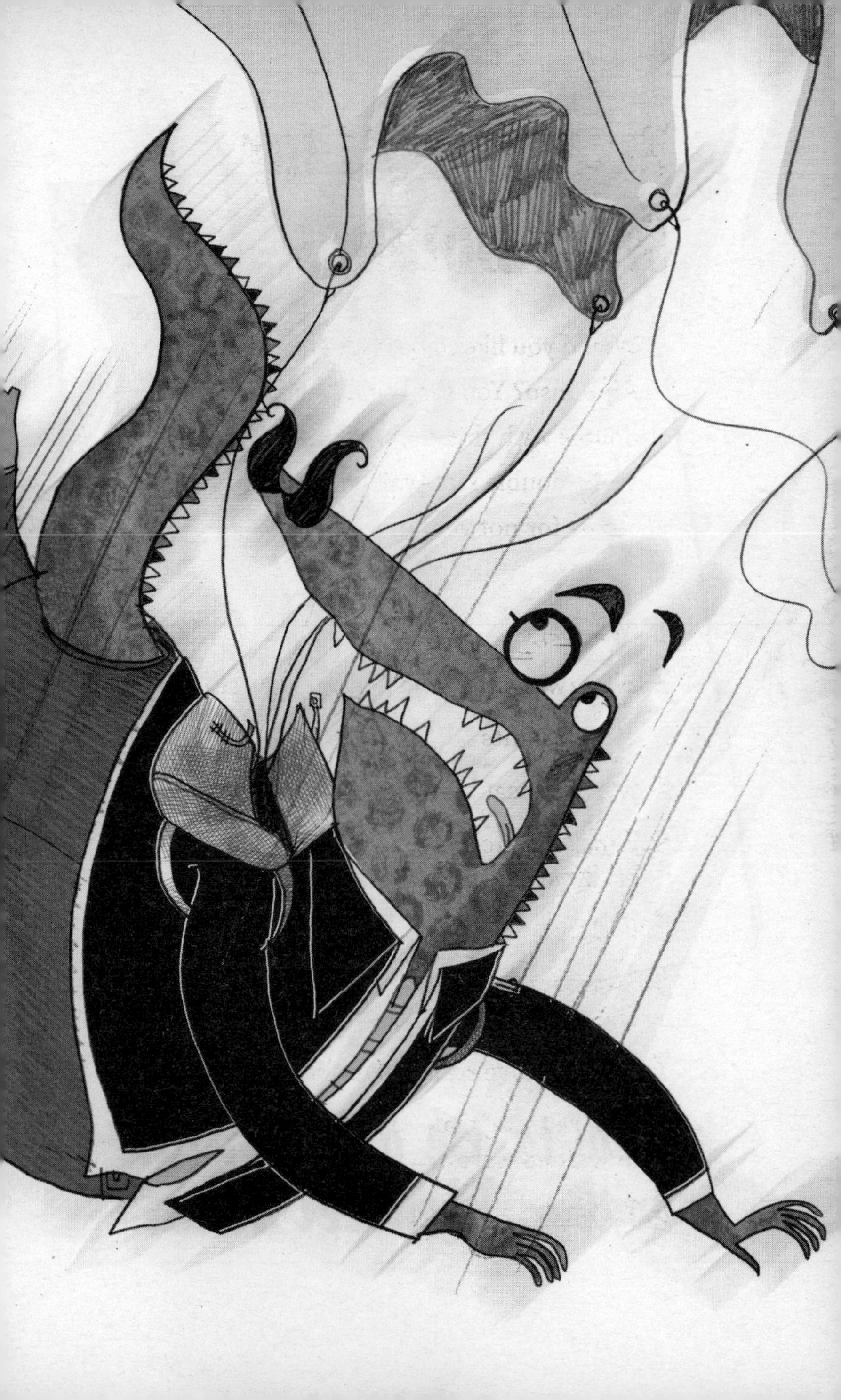

How to Be a Superstar with... Ebenezer Jones

EVER WANTED TO KNOW HOW SUPERSTAR EBENEZER JONES ACHIEVES THAT SUPER-HOT LOOK OF HIS? WELL HERE'S HOW.

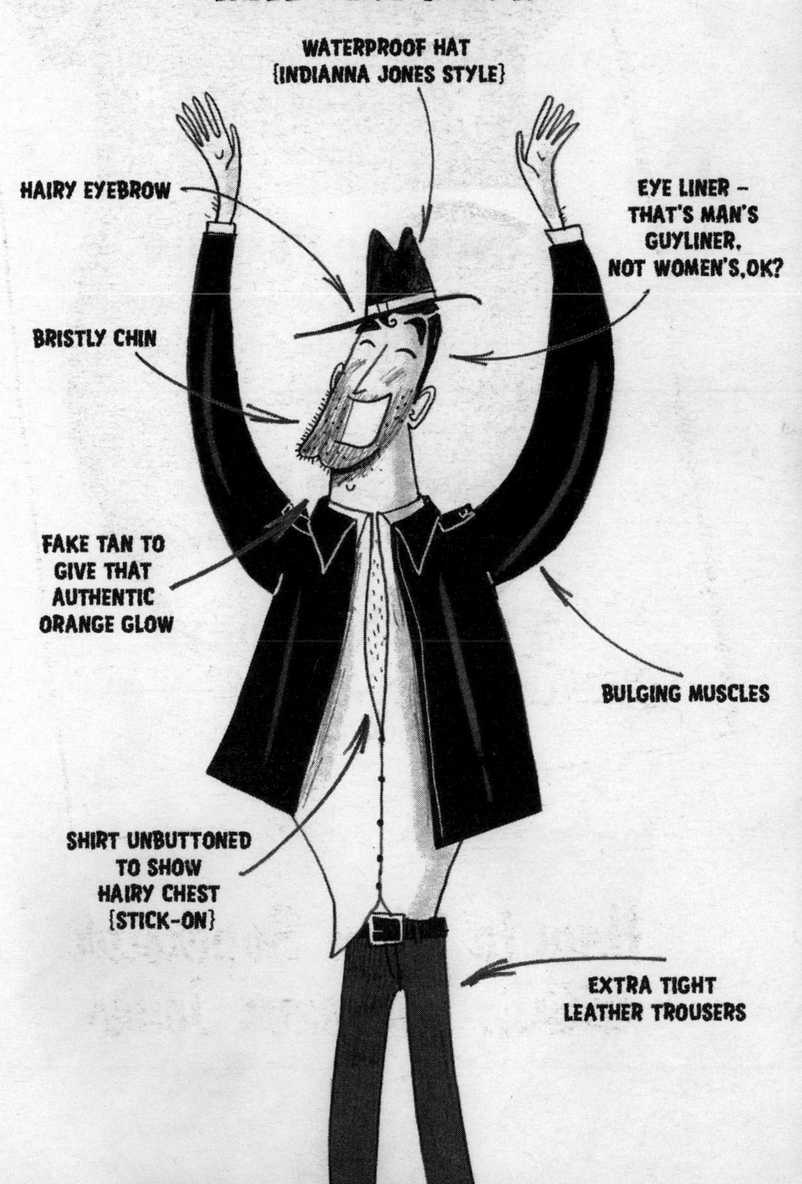

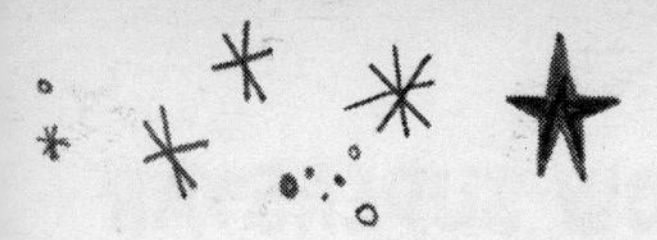

Foxy's Favourites

Favourite Joke

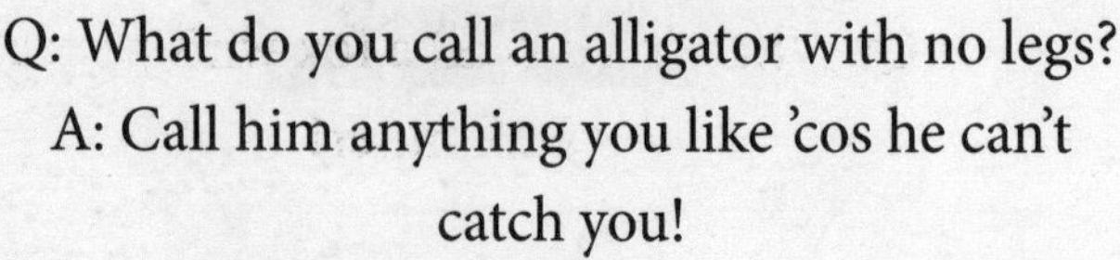

Q: What do you call an alligator with no legs?
A: Call him anything you like 'cos he can't catch you!

Favourite Pastime

Lounging by the pool with a good book and a fruity cocktail. And a slave to fan me with a giant feather.

Favourite Place

Anywhere that's not here!

Favourite Animal

I don't like animals. They smell. And eat all your food. And poop.

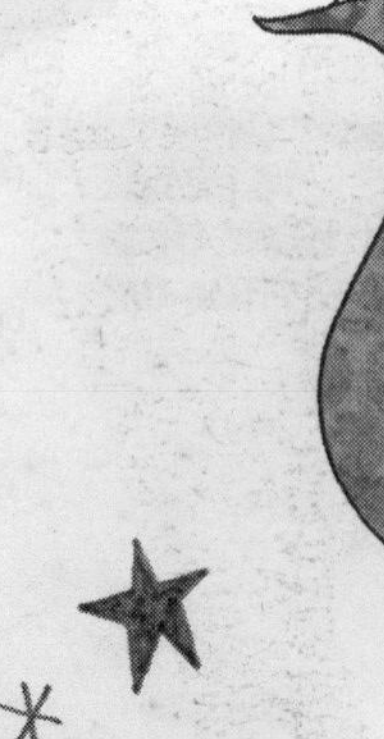

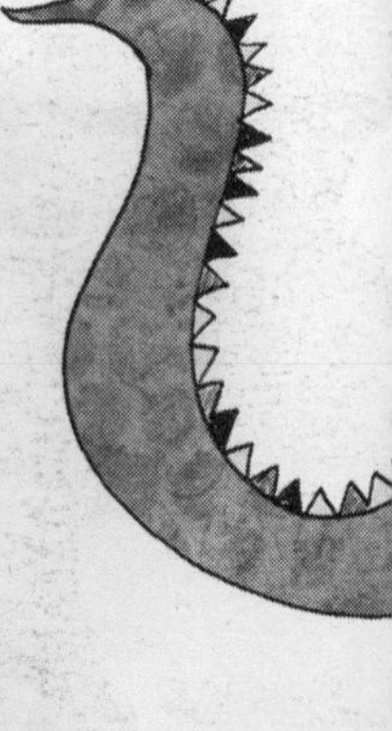

Alphonso's Favourites

Favourite Joke

Q: What do you call a fox with no legs?

A: Dinner!

Favourite Food

Hot dogs. Lots and lots of hot dogs. And doughnuts. With hot dogs inside.

Favourite Shoes

I don't like shoes, they cramp my claws.

Favourite Pastime

Trumping, burping, nose-gardening, picking my teeth and insulting Foxy DuBois.

An Interview with Alphonso

By

ANN RICE-PUDDING

Today I have the pleasure of interviewing Mister Alphonso Alligator, stunt-croc extraordinaire and Jollywood sensation.

Ann: So, Mr Alphonso, what's it like being the number one stunt croc?

Alphonso: Give me a triple bacon sandwich and I'll tell you.

Ann: There you go. Now, can you tell me what is the scariest thing you have ever done?

Alphonso: Gnwarf sluuurp, mugunch, snarrrrfff.

Ann: Oh, err, OK. Perhaps we should wait until you've finished your lunch?

Ann: So. What was it like for you, growing up?

Alphonso: Buuurrrrpppp!

Ann: OK, right. I see. Tell me, where in the world would you most like to go?

Alphonso: To get some pudding. I'm starving. *Long wait while interviewee shovels down three dozen doughnuts, a triple fudge sundae with a cherry on top, and sixteen extra large chocolate éclairs.*

Ann: Gosh, you DO have an appetite! Now, Alphonso, tell me three things you'd like to do before you die. Alphonso?

Err...?

Alphonso: Zzzzzzzzzzzzzzzzz.........

Ann: *sigh*

ALPHONSO ALLIGATOR'S MOUSTACHES FOR ALL OCCASIONS

Stuck for a moustache design? Need a little something for a special occasion? Well, look no further. Alphonso's stunning cut-out-and-wear moustaches are easy to assemble and last for hours.

Simply photocopy this page, cut moustaches out, and attach with sticky tape. Can be used on top lip, chin or ears as required.

1. Everyday moustache
2. Party moustache
3. Stunt moustache
4. Dashingly handsome moustache

2

3

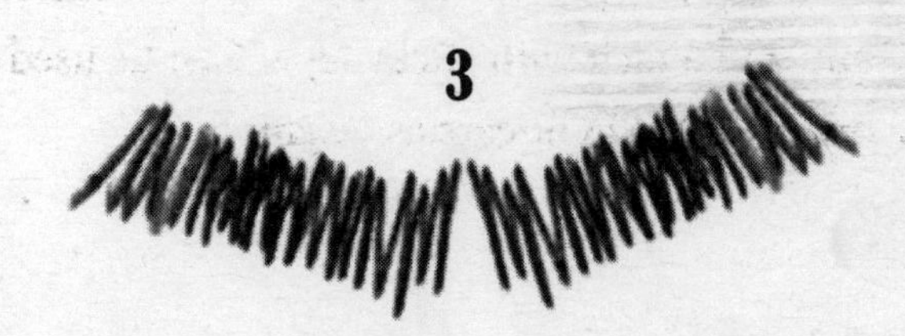

4

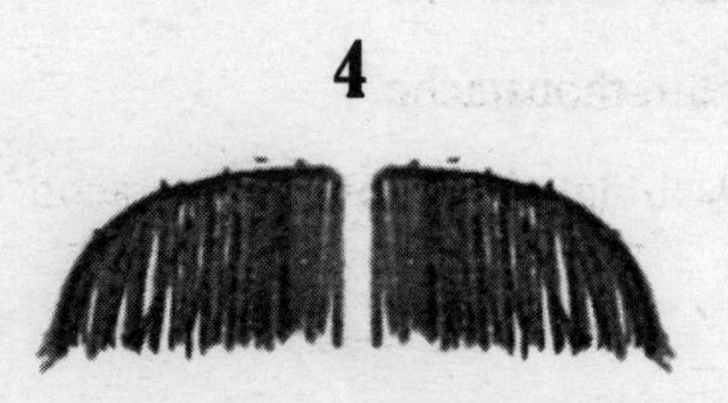